THE GIFT

Based on an old Taoist tale

First Edition
05 04 03 02 01   5 4 3 2 1

Text © 2001 Carol Lynn Pearson
Illustrations © 2001 Kathleen Peterson

Published by
Gibbs Smith, Publisher
P.O. Box 667
Layton, Utah 84041

Order toll-free: (1-800) 748-5439
Website: _www.gibbs-smith.com_
E-mail: _info@gibbs-smith.com_

Edited by Suzanne Taylor
Designed and produced by J. Scott Knudsen, Park City, Utah
Printed and bound in China

Library of Congress Cataloging-in-Publication Data
Pearson, Carol Lynn.
 The gift : a fable for our times/Carol Lynn Pearson ; illustrated by
Kathleen Peterson.— 1st ed.
   p. cm.
ISBN 1-58685-100-4
1. Parent and child—Fiction. I. Title.
PS3566.E227 G54 2001
813'.54—dc21
                    2001001920

THE GIFT

a fable for our times

Carol Lynn Pearson

ILLUSTRATED BY

Kathleen Peterson

GIBBS·SMITH
P
PUBLISHER

SALT LAKE CITY

To Shauna, who has met misfortune with grace and love, giving us all light to see more clearly.

CLP, her cousin
KP, her sister

There was a man who had a son that he loved more than anything in the world. One day he said to his son, "I would give you a gift of the most precious thing I own." And he reached into his pocket and handed to his son something that shone like a diamond.

"What is this?" asked the son as he fingered the shining thing.

"Something for the dark times," said the father, "something to help you see. Keep it in the pocket over your heart, and never lose it."

P uzzled, the son put the shining thing in his pocket, then said, "But, Father, what I would really like to have is that horse over there in the pasture, the gleaming black one that runs as fast as the wind. Could I have that horse, Father?"

The father thought a moment, then said, "You may have that horse, my son."

"Oh, thank you, Father," said the young man. "This is the most excellent horse! I am so fortunate!"

Smiling, the father placed the reins in his son's hand and said, "We will see."

Horse

The young man spent many happy days riding with his companions through the fields and forests and over the mountains and into the valleys.

But one morning he found that his horse had leapt over the fence and run away. "Oh, no!" cried the young man. "My excellent horse is gone! Oh, I am so unfortunate!"

The father put a hand on his son's shoulder and said, "We will see."

A few days later, the young man was awakened by the sound of thundering hooves. He ran out to see his horse leading a herd of twelve wild mustangs toward the pasture.

"Look, Father," he cried, as he opened the gate and drove them in. "Now I have *many* horses! How fortunate I am!"

The father joined him and, seeing the prancing, neighing horses, said to his son, "We will see."

Fortunate

The following morning, as the son was attempting to ride one of the new horses, the stallion bucked wildly, throwing the young man onto the ground and breaking his leg.

"Ah!" he cried through his pain as the bone was set and the leg bound tightly, "I wish the wild horses were still in the mountain! Ah, I am so unfortunate!"

The father made some good cabbage soup and brought it to his son, and gently said, "We will see."

Soup

That afternoon the King's soldiers came through the village, conscripting all the young men into the army to march to the front and fight the enemy. The only young man they did not take was the one with the broken leg.

"Ah!" said the young man, smiling in relief, for he never wanted to march to the front and fight the enemy, "Ah! I am so fortunate!"

The father watched the last of the soldiers disappear over the horizon, and said to his son, "We will see."

Fortunate

In the following days and weeks and months, the young man became very lonely. All of his comrades were gone to war. He watched the horizon for their return, but to no avail. "There is no one to be my friend," he lamented to his father. "Oh, I am so unfortunate!"

The father looked over at the village square and said, "We will see."

Soon every young woman for miles around was making eyes at the young man, for indeed he was the only available man in the village.

"Why, look, Father," said the young man. "I can have my pick of all the girls! I can choose the most beautiful to be my wife!"

And he did. He fell in love with the girl with the shinlest hair and the clearest skin and the brightest eyes and the most stunning smile. Swooning, he looked at his bride-to-be and said to his father, "Is she not the most beautiful girl in the land? Indeed I am the most fortunate of men!"

The father held out his arms to his lovely new daughter-in-law and said to his son, "We will see."

Fortunate

Before the month was out, the young man discovered that his new wife was not only beautiful, she was also spoiled and self-centered, and chose not to sully her soft hands with dusting the house or feeding the pigs.

Eventually the young man confided his unhappiness to his father, saying, "What a poor choice I made in a wife! Oh, I am so unfortunate!"

The father smiled and put an arm around his son and said, "We will see."

The young man worked very hard to see past his wife's beauty, and also past her spoiledness, her self-centeredness, and her laziness. He found things inside of her that he did not know were there, things that *she* did not know were there, things that no one had looked for before.

And as he did so, he found things within himself that he did not know were there.

Love

The young man and his wife created together a life of happiness and kindness and patience and forgiveness, and they negotiated well how often the house had to be dusted and who would feed the pigs. They were blessed with children, and their home was filled with peace and harmony and laughter and love.

Often the young man's father came to visit, and his son said to him, "Ah, Father! Look at my wonderful family! I am the most fortunate of all men!"

The father kissed the forehead of the sweet grandchild sitting on his lap, and said, "We will see."

Fortunate

One day after many years had passed, the young man came to his father's house weeping. "Oh, Father!" he said. "I am most miserable! My eldest daughter, whom I love more than anything in the world, wants to leave home and go with her disorderly friends into the city! She will not listen to my wisdom, and I know that nothing but evil will come of it. Oh, I am so unfortunate! And so is *she!*"

The father considered for a bit, then said gently, "My son, have you given her the gift?"

"The gift?" asked the son, puzzled.

"In your pocket."

Faith

The young man reached into the pocket over his heart and brought out something that shone like a diamond.

"Ah," he said, trying to remember. "Something for the dark times? Something to help me see?"

"Of course," smiled the father. "To see that all things *simply are*, and that all things work together for good."

"I have had this all along?"

"How else would you have dared to ride a horse again, or to discover the true beauty within your wife, or to bring children into this world? Is it in your daughter's pocket as well?"

The young man thought a moment, and tears dropped onto the shining thing in his hand. "It will be before sunset," he said.

The father embraced his son and held him long. "Keep some for yourself," he said. "You will need it. I have that on good authority from my father and his father and all the fathers back and back and back to the First Father who let a child leave home."

Respect

"It is very bright, isn't it?" the young man said, as he fingered the shining thing.

"Very bright," agreed the father, looking at his son as if they shared a sweet secret.

The young man shifted his gaze. "The city is very dark, isn't it?" he said.

"Very dark," nodded the father.

"But one day...one day...." The son spoke hopefully, lifting the shining thing and looking through it at the distant city.

"…we will see."